P9-DDB-056

Boo
to a goose

Mem Fox
pictures by David Miller

Dial Books for Young Readers  New York

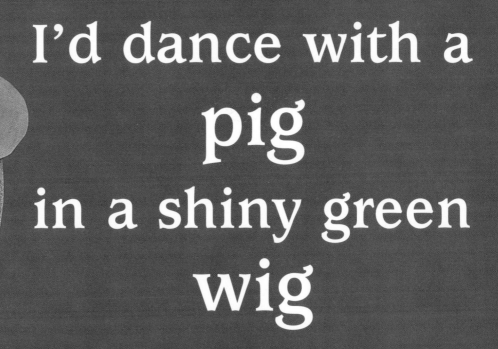

I'd dance with a
pig
in a shiny green
wig

But I wouldn't say

"*BOO!*"

to a goose.

I'd ride on a 'roo
to Kalamazoo

But I wouldn't say "BOO!" to a goose.

I'd dive from a
mountain
right into a
fountain

But I wouldn't say

"BOO!"

to a goose.

I'd play with a snake

I'd gobble up
snails
from smelly old
pails

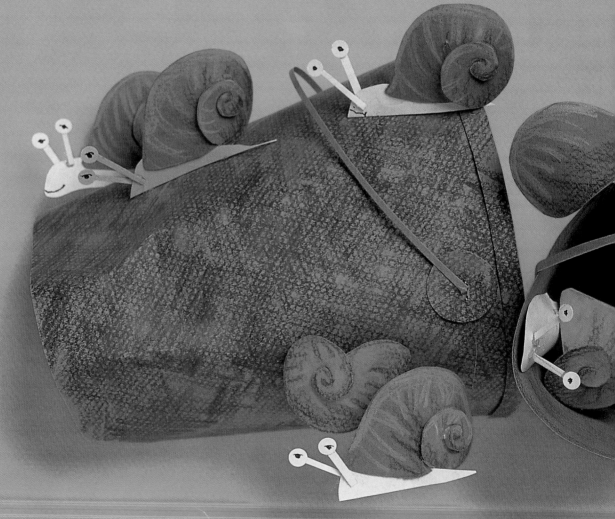

I'd take a long
walk
from here to
New York

But I wouldn't say

"BOO!" to a goose.

I'd swim with a **whale** without going **pale**

But I wouldn't say
"BOO!"
to a goose.

I'd feed my **pajamas**

to giant piranhas

But I wouldn't say

"BOO!"

to a goose.

I'd walk down the
street
with balloons on my
feet

But I wouldn't say "BOO!" to a goose.

I'd dye my hair **yellow**
and make Grandma
bellow

But I wouldn't say

I'd walk on my
knees
past a hive full of
bees

But I wouldn't say

"BOO!"

to a goose.

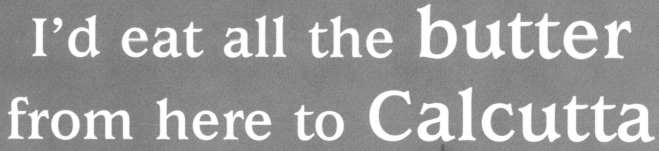

I'd eat all the **butter** from here to **Calcutta**

But I wouldn't say

"BOO!" to a goose.

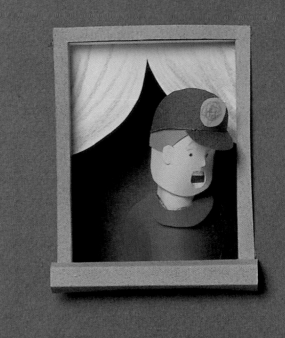

I'd skip across town with my pants hanging down

But I wouldn't say

"BOO!"

to a goose.

I'd do all these things quite bravely – you'd see!

But I wouldn't say "BOO!" to one goose or three

because...

a goose once said

"BOO!"

to me!

FOR JÜRGEN, AT LAST
M.F.

FOR SYLVIA
D.M.

First published in the United States 1998 by Dial Books for Young Readers
A Division of Penguin Books USA Inc.
375 Hudson Street • New York, New York 10014

Published in Australia and New Zealand 1996 by Hodder Headline Australia Pty Limited,
A member of the Hodder Headline Group
Text copyright © 1996 by Mem Fox • Pictures copyright © 1996 by David Miller
All rights reserved • Printed in Hong Kong on acid-free paper
First Edition
1 3 5 7 9 10 8 6 4 2

Library of Congress Cataloging in Publication Data
Fox, Mem, date.
Boo to a goose/Mem Fox; pictures by David Miller.—1st ed.
p. cm.
Summary: A boy relates a long list of things he would do before he'd say boo to a goose.
ISBN 0-8037-2274-5
[1. Geese—Fiction. 2. Stories in rhyme. 3. Humorous stories.]
I. Miller, David, date, ill. II. Title. PZ8.3.F8245Bo 1998 [E]—dc21 96-54225 CIP AC

The art for this book was created with paper sculpture.